ILLUSTRATED CLASSICS

GREEK MYTHS

ADAPTED BY SAVIOUR PIROTTA

ILLUSTRATED BY

LEO HARTAS · AMANDA SARTOR

MIKE LOVE · GERALD KELLEY

Sandy Creek
NEW YORK

Jason and the Golden Fleece

For as long as he could remember, Jason had lived with his guardian Chiron, a minotaur, in the mountains. But now he had grown into a man and was ready to leave.

"There are important things I must tell you before you depart," said Chiron. "You are the heir to the kingdom of Iolcos. Your parents were murdered by your uncle, Pelias, who stole the throne."

Chiron unwrapped a bundle to reveal a pair of golden sandals. "These belonged to your father."

Jason put the sandals on. "I shall avenge my parents' death and reclaim my throne," he said.

On his way to Iolcos, Jason had to cross a river. He waded through the deep, churning water, the current sweeping away one of his new sandals.

When he reached the gates of Iolcos, the guards pointed and stared at him.

"He's wearing only one sandal," they gasped.

When Jason got to the palace, a crowd gathered around him, mesmerized by his remaining sandal.

"Please ignore my people," said King Pelias. "There is a silly prophecy that I will be dethroned by a man who comes to Iolcos wearing only one sandal."

"It may well come true," said Jason. "I am your nephew. I have come to reclaim my father's kingdom."

"I will hand back the crown if you prove you are worthy of it," said Pelias. "Bring me the Golden Fleece!"

A Great Ship

Everyone in Greece had heard of the fabled Golden Fleece, a magic talisman that brought good luck and riches to anyone who owned it. It was said that it hung on the branches of a sacred oak tree in Colchis, a country at the edge of the world. The fleece was guarded by a giant serpent that never slept. Many had gone in search of it, never to return.

That night, Jason prayed to Athena, and she spoke to him in a dream.

"Instruct Argus, a ship builder in Iolcos, to build you a ship. I shall guide you safely to Colchis and back. I have summoned heroes from all over Greece to be your crew and help you in your quest."

Jason did as Athena asked, and within the month the ship was ready. Jason called it the *Argo* after its builder. Famous heroes from far and wide came to join its crew, including the poet Orpheus, who wrote beautiful songs.

"He takes artists with him instead of warriors," sneered King Pelias when he came to see the *Argo*.
"And how is the fool going to move his ship from the yard to the harbor?"

As he spoke, Orpheus started singing. The *Argo* sailed out of the yard as if it was carried on invisible waves.

In no time at all, it had reached the water's edge. The crowd cheered and Jason stood at the prow.
"All hail the Argonauts!" he shouted.

Colchis

A few days later, the *Argo* docked at Colchis.

"What is that strange ship in my harbor?" King Aietes asked his daughter, Medea.

"That is the *Argo*. They have come for the fleece," replied Medea, who had magical powers.

"Many have attempted to take the fleece," laughed the king. "These men will fail, too. I will throw a feast to welcome them, and it will be their last!"

"Have you come to find the Golden Fleece?" Aietes asked Jason later as they ate.

"I cannot lie to you," replied Jason. "I have."

"My ancestors brought the fleece to Colchis many years ago," said Aietes. "But I'll let you take it in return for a favor."

He threw a small bag on the table. "The Golden Fleece hangs on the branches of a sacred oak. The soil around it is very fertile. Plant the seeds in this bag for me so that other sacred trees may grow."

After the banquet, Medea approached Jason.

"My father means to trick you," she said. "The seeds in the bag are dragons' teeth. They will kill you."

"Why do you tell me this?" asked Jason.

"Take me with you and I will help you," said Medea.

Jason accepted the offer and Medea spoke quickly. "When the dragons' teeth sprout tomorrow, take off your helmet and hurl it at whatever comes out of the ground. I shall wait for you close by."

A Skeleton Army

At sunset the next day, Jason made his way to the sacred oak. He plunged his hand into the bag that King Aietes had given him and pulled out a handful of dragons' teeth. He carefully sowed them in a line, covering them with soil.

A few moments later, the ground began to shake, as if a great earthquake was taking place. Jason stepped back in surprise. Suddenly, the tips of spears began to rise out of the soil. Behind them followed helmets and pale bleached faces with blank hooded eyes.

Jason watched in horror as an army of skeletons leaped out at him, surrounding him with sharp, deadly looking spears. He raised his sword and slashed it through the air. The warriors could not see, but locating their victim by the sound of his sword, they started to hiss like snakes and close in on Jason.

In the distance, Jason heard Medea shout.

"Jason, the helmet!"

Jason took off his helmet and hurled it at the skeleton closest to him. The skeleton warriors stopped in their tracks. Together, they turned toward the helmet and, a moment later, began to attack each other, hacking and lunging with their spears and swords.

Before long, the ground was littered with piles of skulls and bones.

The skeleton army had been conquered, and Jason had triumphed again!

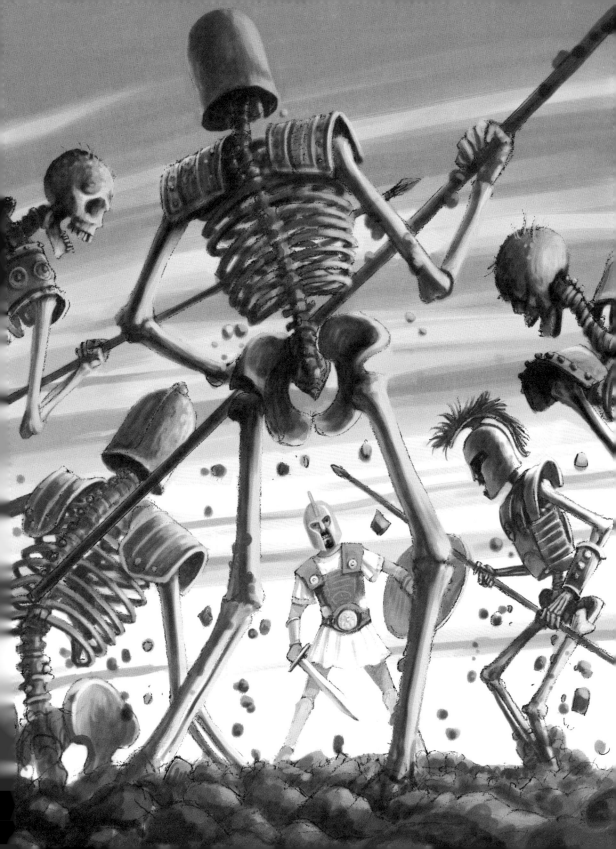

The Golden Fleece

It was dark now, and the Golden Fleece, hanging from the sacred oak, glinted in the moonlight. Below it, the serpent slithered menacingly around the trunk.

As promised, Medea had come to the grove, and she had brought Orpheus with her. They all heard a loud hiss, and the serpent's head appeared around the tree trunk. Its forked tongue, longer than Jason's sword, flickered. Hiding behind a nearby tree, the poet started singing a quiet song that seemed to calm the serpent.

Medea tiptoed up to the sacred oak and, chanting a spell, waved a twig around the serpent's head. The serpent's eyes closed and its head fell to the ground.

Medea whispered loudly. "Hurry, Jason, the spell only lasts a short while. Get the fleece."

Jason clambered up the tree and lifted the Golden Fleece with the tip of his sword. Below him, the serpent whose body was coiled tightly in rings around the tree, stirred. Medea's spell was wearing off. Jason jumped to the ground and the three of them ran out of the grove. Behind them, the serpent began to hiss angrily again. Defeated, it turned on itself and began to eat its own tail.

By sunrise, the *Argo* had slipped out of the harbor at Colchis. Medea and Jason stood together at the helm. Above them, draped over the sail, was the Golden Fleece, shimmering in the morning sun.

The Argonauts cheered. "To the *Argo* and to Jason, the future king of Iolcos."

Perseus and Medusa

Dictys, the fisherman, lived on the island of Seriphos. Early one morning he was returning home when he saw a large chest washed up on the beach. He opened it to find a sleeping woman inside with a baby in her arms.

"I am Queen Danae, and this is my son, Perseus," said the woman to Dictys and his wife, Clymene, when she woke up. "The oracle told my father, King Acrisius of Argo, that his grandson would grow up to kill him. So he locked us in this chest and threw us into the sea."

"You are welcome to live with us," said Clymene. "You'll be safe here."

Dictys's older brother was the king of Seriphos, a stern man named Polydectes. News of Danae's arrival soon reached him. He came to visit, and the moment he set eyes on Danae, he wanted to marry her.

Danae did not want to marry anyone. All she wanted to do was raise Perseus. "I will consider your kind proposal when my son is older," she said to Polydectes.

Years passed, and Perseus grew into a young man. Polydectes still visited Danae, but one day, he told her he was going to marry a princess from another island.

"Congratulations," said Perseus. "If I had money, I would buy you a wedding gift."

"There is a gift you could bring me," said Polydectes.

"Just say the word," said Perseus foolishly.

"Bring me the head of Medusa!" replied the king.

Gifts from the Gods

"It is a trick!" said Danae when she heard what had happened. "Medusa can turn a man to stone with one glance. This talk of marrying another princess is a lie. You will die, and without you to protect me, Polydectes will make me marry him."

"You must pray to the gods for counsel," said Clymene, who had been listening to the conversation.

"Yes," said Perseus. "I shall seek Athena's help."

He went out to an altar he had built in the orchard.

"Who walks among the sacred trees?" called a voice, and a beautiful woman stepped out in Perseus's path.

"I am Perseus."

"I am Athena. I have something that will protect you from Medusa the gorgon." The goddess held out a shield. "When you approach her, do not look into her eyes. Instead, gaze at her reflection in this."

A graceful man with a lyre appeared next to Athena. "I am the god Hermes," he said. "I, too, have a gift."

He held out a dagger made of adamantine. "This is the only metal that can pierce a gorgon's scales."

"I thank you both," said Perseus, accepting the gifts. "But where shall I find Medusa?"

"Only the nymphs know," replied Athena. "The gray women, sisters to the gorgons, will help you find them."

Hermes put out his hands and a pair of winged sandals appeared in them. "Put these on. They will take you wherever you ask them."

The Gray Sisters

"Sandals, take me to the gray women," said Perseus. The wings carried Perseus for miles before he landed at a hut in a dark valley. An old woman came to the door.

"Who comes near?"

"A traveler," replied Perseus.

A second woman arrived. "Do I hear a man, Deino?"

"Aye, Enyo, you do."

The first woman looked Perseus up and down with one glassy eye. Her other eye socket was empty.

"Let me see him," cried the second woman, whose eye sockets were both empty.

A third woman appeared. She too was sightless.

"There's a man at our door, Pemphredo," said Deino.

"Where can I find the nymphs?" asked Perseus.

"That," snapped Pemphredo, "we will never divulge. Pass me the eye, Deino. Let me see this stranger."

Perseus realized that the three sisters had only one eye between them. He darted forward and snatched it.

The three women gasped. "Give us back our eye!"

"First, tell me where I can find the nymphs."

The women knew Perseus had them cornered. Without the eye, they would live in darkness.

"You'll find them by the River Styx in the underworld," cried Pemphredo. "Now return our eye."

"Here it is," said Perseus, and he dropped the eye in Pemphredo's hand.

On the Banks of the River

"Take me to the River Styx," commanded Perseus. The sandals carried Perseus out of the valley and deep within the bowels of the Earth. He felt himself falling gently, the wings on the sandals beating against his ankles. At last they set him down close to a river, where three beautiful creatures in moss-green robes were standing. They were the nymphs.

"Welcome, stranger," said one of them.

"Yes, welcome. It has been a long time since we last saw a mortal," said the second.

"Yes, a very long time. Welcome. And such a handsome mortal. A prince no doubt!" added the third.

"I've been set the task of slaying Medusa the gorgon," said Perseus. "Will you help me?"

"We are duty-bound to help anyone who finds us," replied the nymphs. "We have useful gifts for you."

One of them held out a hunting bag. "When you cut off Medusa's head, put it in this. No other bag will do, for the gorgons' blood burns through everything."

"You will not be able to cut off Medusa's head unless you wear this," said the second nymph, giving Perseus a helmet. "Put it on and it will make you invisible."

"I have no gift to offer, but I shall tell you where the gorgons live," added the third nymph. "Seek them at the foot of the Black Mountain and approach with courage. It is only with courage that you will get safely through your adventure."

Face to Face with Medusa

"To the Black Mountain," Perseus ordered the sandals, and they carried him out of the underworld and across a scorching desert to a large, gloomy cavern.

The entrance was half-blocked with boulders. Flying closer, Perseus realized they were not rocks at all, but people turned to stone by the piercing gaze of the gorgons' eyes. He put on the helmet of invisibility.

From inside the cavern came the sound of the gorgons' voices. "Medusa is late for dinner. She must be very hungry by now," said Stheno, Medusa's first sister.

"Yes, and her snakes must be ravenous, too," said Euryale, the second sister. "Oh, here she is now."

Perseus felt a rush of wind behind him as Medusa flew into the cave on her golden wings. The venomous snakes on her head squirmed and hissed angrily, and the scales on her body glinted in the darkness. Perseus closed his eyes and waited until the gorgons had eaten and fallen asleep. Then he stole up on them, his eyes fixed firmly on their reflection in his shield. The adamantine dagger sliced through the air, and a second later, Medusa's head was rolling across the cave floor.

The other two gorgons, Stheno and Euryale, awoken by the hiss of Medusa's snakes, leaped up and screeched angrily. They peered about them, but they could not see Perseus in his magic helmet. He flew out of the cave, Medusa's head tucked safely in the hunting bag.

A Present for King Polydectes

The winged sandals carried Perseus back to Seriphos. He arrived at Polydectes' palace halfway through a banquet. The king, celebrating his imminent marriage to Danae, looked up from his wine cup.

"So you have not found Medusa after all," he scoffed.

"I promised you her head," said Perseus, "and I always keep my promises."

"Did you hear that?" Polydectes roared with laughter. "The young hero has vanquished the gorgon."

Perseus looked around at the guests in the hall. "If any of you are my friends," he warned, "shut your eyes."

Most of the men obeyed right away. Perseus opened the bag and pulled out Medusa's head, holding it high. King Polydectes had only a moment to notice the dead eyes of the gorgon . . . then his wine cup fell to the floor as he turned to stone.

Perseus returned to Dictys's home to see his mother. Later that night, he stole out to the orchard and placed the gods' gifts at the altar.

One by one, the gifts disappeared until only Athena's shield was left. Then Athena herself appeared. "Well done, Perseus," she said. "You have rid the world of a monster."

She held up the shield, where an image of Medusa's face had appeared. "From now on," said the goddess, "the gorgon's gaze will not harm. Instead, it will protect anyone who looks upon it and offers sacrifice to me."

Theseus and the Minotaur

Queen Aethra looked at her son with worry in her eyes. "Theseus, tell me, have they been teasing you at the gymnasium again?"

"They say I have no father," said her son. "A man without a father is no better than a slave, even if he lives in a palace. Your priests insist that Poseidon himself is my father…"

"Poseidon is your godfather," said Queen Aethra. "Sometimes the gods adopt a favorite mortal. But perhaps it is time you knew who your real father is."

She led Theseus to an orchard. "When I was your age, a king visited Troezen. He was childless and very badly wanted an heir. I took pity on him. But before you were born, he was called away. There was trouble in his kingdom. The night before he left, he brought me here and hid some precious things under a giant stone."

By now the queen had stopped near a boulder. "Your father said, 'When my son is strong enough to lift this, let him retrieve the objects under it. Then send him to me.' Your father is King Aegeus of Athens. Now see if you can lift the stone."

Theseus grabbed one end of the boulder with both hands and, using all his strength, managed to push it away. There was a small hole in the ground below it. He reached in and drew out a package. Inside was a pair of leather sandals and a short sword with a jeweled hilt.

Medea's Plan

Theseus set off to Athens the next morning on foot. On the way, he ran into many robbers. He vanquished them all, so that by the time he reached Athens, his fame had already spread to the city.

Theseus's father, King Aegeus, had a new queen. She was a witch named Medea. Curious about the stranger, she used her magic powers to conjure up his image in a water basin. She was horrified to see that he looked very much like the king! Her heart skipped a beat. Did Aegeus have a secret son? Medea didn't like that at all. She wanted her own son, if she ever had one, to be the king's one and only heir.

"I take it you have invited the young traveler to a banquet," she said to Aegeus.

"Yes," he replied. "We must honor our visitors."

"The man means to murder you," said Medea. She handed him a vial. "Put this poison in his wine."

Theseus was telling the tale of his journey when Aegeus tried to put his plan into action.

"Some more wine, Theseus?" Aegeus asked, dropping the poison into the cup. Just then, Theseus took out his sword to cut some cheese, and Aegeus turned pale!

"Where did you get that sword?"

"In the very spot where you buried it," replied Theseus. "I am your son. To your health, Father!"

Theseus raised his cup to drink but Aegeus knocked it out of his hand.

King Minos and a Crown

That night, father and son talked and talked. "I would like to celebrate your arrival," said Aegeus, "but, alas, King Minos of Crete reaches Athens tomorrow."

A few years before, Minos's son had been killed in an accident at the Athenian games. In revenge, he had demanded seven young men and seven young women from Athens every year. They were fed to Minos's other son, a half-man, half-bull called the Minotaur.

"Let me destroy this monster, Father," said Theseus.

"I will send you to Crete with a heavy heart," said Aegeus. "If you succeed in killing the Minotaur, hoist a white sail on your ship returning home. But if you die, let your sailors hoist a black one. That way I will know I have lost you."

Theseus left Athens a few days later with the other prisoners. King Minos took an instant dislike to him.

"Is it true Poseidon is your adopted father?" he taunted, plucking a ring from his finger and hurling it into the sea. "If it really is true, return that to me."

Theseus dived into the sea. Peering down, Minos thought he saw Theseus being carried by dolphins into an underwater palace! Minos thought he must be imagining things. Soon, Theseus climbed back onto the ship. He was carrying the ring and a jeweled crown.

"It was given to me by Poseidon's wife," said Theseus, "as proof that Poseidon really is my godfather."

Princess Ariadne's Promise

In Crete, Theseus and the Athenians were locked in the dungeons to await their fate. One night, Theseus heard someone whispering.

"I am Princess Ariadne, King Minos's daughter."

He looked up to see a young woman through the bars of his cell. "I can help you defeat the Minotaur," she said. "If you promise to take me away with you."

She held out a ball of string. "Tie this to the door handle in the labyrinth. Let it out behind you as you walk. When you have killed the Minotaur, wind it up again and it will lead you back to the entrance."

She held out a second object, a dagger. "No ordinary weapon will pierce the Minotaur's skin. You will need this blade made of adamantine to destroy him."

The next day, Theseus offered to be the first victim in the labyrinth. Tying the string to the door as Ariadne had instructed, he ventured into the darkness. Suddenly, he came face to face with the Minotaur. The beast towered above him, steam flaring from his nostrils.

Theseus drew his dagger. The Minotaur chuckled, unafraid of the weapon he knew was useless against his skin. The two circled each other in the darkness. Then Theseus leaped forward, and the beast gasped in pain as the knife plunged into him, killing him. Theseus went back to the entrance where Ariadne was waiting for him.

"There's a secret passage that can get us past the guards outside," she whispered. "Follow me."

A Wedding

Ariadne had planned Theseus's escape very well. There was a ship waiting in the harbor, with a crew. The other prisoners from Athens were already on board.

"You have saved our lives," said Theseus to Ariadne, as they slipped out of the harbor under cover of darkness. He placed the crown that he had been given by Poseidon's wife upon her head. "I would like you to be my queen. Will you marry me? We are coming to an island called Naxos soon. We could stop there for our wedding."

Ariadne accepted, and a little later, the ship dropped anchor at Naxos.

"It is the custom here," said the priest in the local temple, "that the bride purifies herself at our sacred spring before her wedding."

Ariadne departed for the spring with some priestesses. By sunset she had not come back. Theseus was starting to worry and wanted to go and look for her, but then a priestess approached.

"We were bathing in the sacred waters," she said, "when a golden chariot appeared out of nowhere. Standing in it was a tall man holding a staff entwined with ivy. He smiled at Ariadne and she climbed into the chariot as if under a spell. The tall man said to me, 'I have come to collect my bride before she is wed to another. Tell Theseus that the god Dionysus himself will marry Ariadne.' And then the chariot disappeared into thin air!"

White Sail, Black Sail

A heartbroken Theseus sailed on to Athens without Ariadne. As they approached the harbor, the captain said, "We are nearly home. Shall we raise a sail? It will get us there faster than rowing."

"Do as you please," mumbled Theseus, without even opening his eyes. He was still grieving for Ariadne.

"Let him rest," the captain said to the sailors. "We'll wake him before we enter the harbor."

The sailors hoisted the first sail they found in the hold. They had not been told about Theseus's agreement with his father.

King Aegeus was watching out for Theseus's ship from a lookout above the harbor.

"Can you see the ship clearly now?" he asked his slave. "Is the sail black or white?"

The slave struggled to speak. "I am afraid it is black," he whispered.

"Black?" cried the king. "Then my son is dead!"

And a moment later, he stepped over the edge of the cliff into the sea.

Theseus was crowned king the very next day. Under his rule, Athens grew from a small city into a dazzling empire. Its name inspires awe to this very day, and Theseus became a hero to the people. His name was blessed, and his brave deeds were recounted in poems through the ages. He is known as the greatest king that Athens ever had!

The Twelve Tasks of Heracles

The gods looked down from Mount Olympus.

"Brave Heracles is arriving home from battle," said Zeus to Hera.

"Brave? He's nothing but a brute," scoffed Hera, who detested Heracles. "He acts as if he were an immortal!"

Hera made sure no other gods were looking and flung a hot coal from the fire toward Heracles. The warrior was blinded for a moment. When his vision cleared, he could see his house was on fire.

Wolves were leaping around in the flames. Heracles drew his club, and moments later the wolves were dead.

"Master!" called a slave, running out of the house.

Heracles looked up. His house was not on fire. His eyes had tricked him. And the bodies on the ground were not wolves. He'd killed his own wife and children.

On Mount Olympus, Hera laughed. Her cruel trick had worked; Heracles was a murderer now, not a hero.

The hero was beside himself with grief. What could he do to make up for his terrible mistake?

"You must visit your cousin, King Eurystheus of Tiryns," suggested the oracle. "He will give you ten tasks. Do them and you will be happy again."

But Hera spoke to Eurystheus in a dream. "You must give Heracles ten fearsome tasks as I instruct you . . ."

"Your first task is . . ." said Eurystheus when Heracles arrived, "to kill the Nemean lion."

The Nemean Lion

The Nemean lion was no ordinary creature. It was a hideous monster, the son of a dragon and a snake, which gobbled up unsuspecting travelers. It haunted the countryside near a city called Nemea.

For weeks, Heracles looked for the lion in the wilderness with no success. He set traps near water holes. He lay in wait for it outside its lair, but the beast always eluded him. Then one morning, while he was washing in a stream, he heard a growl behind him. He looked up and saw the lion glaring at him from the banks. Heracles fired an arrow at it. The lion did not even flinch. The arrow merely bounced off its thick fur and fell to the ground. The lion dipped its head to drink from the stream and, taking his chance, Heracles picked up a large rock and hurled it at the beast.

"Ha!" he shouted.

The rock hit the lion right on the head. The beast roared angrily, fixed its red eyes on Heracles, and came straight at him.

Heracles stopped for a split second to pick up his mighty club, then bolted toward the lion's den and ran straight into it! The lion followed. But now Heracles had the upper hand. At close quarters, not even a monster could match his strength. He attacked and defeated the lion with his bare hands, not even needing the club.

Later that night, he returned to Eurystheus's palace wearing a gleaming new cloak made of lion fur.

The Hydra

Heracles's next task was to destroy the Hydra, a serpent with nine heads that lived in a lake. Its blood was said to be deadly poison. Get one drop of it on your skin and you would die in a moment.

Heracles took a friend to help him, a warrior named Iolaus. The two lit a fire on the shores of the Hydra's lake, hoping to cook some food.

But no sooner was the fire burning, than the water started to bubble and a serpent's head, followed by eight more, rose out of the water. The Hydra clambered out of the lake, the ground shaking under its feet.

Heracles pulled out his sword, and a moment later, one of the monster's heads fell to the ground.

"One down," he called to Iolaus. "Eight to go."

But he was wrong. A moment later, two new heads grew out of the torn neck. Now the hydra had ten heads!

"Iolaus," shouted Heracles, breathing hard. "Dip a torch into the fire. When I chop off another head, hold the flame to the wound. It think it will prevent more heads from growing."

He lashed out with his sword again, cutting off another head. Iolaus jumped at the flailing neck and held the flaming torch firmly against the wound. The trick worked. No new heads appeared.

The sun was rising when the monster's last head hit the ground. It was the main one, twice as big as all the others. The Hydra fell limp. It was dead.

The Amazons

Heracles's next task was to catch a deer with golden antlers. Then a deadly wild boar. After that, he cleaned the stables of a king, who gave Heracles a bag of gold.

Next, Heracles had to kill a flock of birds that ate human flesh. He captured a bull that breathed fire. He tamed a herd of monster horses! And he stole a herd of oxen from a giant with three bodies. He was invincible!

"He'll be no match for the Amazons," laughed Eurystheus. "I'll send him to fetch their queen's belt."

The Amazons were fierce women. Their ruler, Queen Hippolyte, had a magic belt.

Heracles sailed to the island where the Amazons lived. Queen Hippolyte came to meet him as he docked. She invited him and his men to a feast.

"I cannot lie to you," Heracles said to Hippolyte. "I have been sent to steal your belt."

"People believe it makes me invincible," said the queen. "But it is my courage that makes me so."

That night at the banquet, Hera, who was disguised as an old woman, approached the palace guards. "Your queen is about to be kidnapped," she warned.

The Amazon guards at once stormed the banqueting hall. Heracles and his men were taken by surprise, but they gathered their wits and fought back. Heracles raised his bow, and a moment later, Queen Hippolyte fell. Heracles snatched her belt and fled the island.

The Golden Apples

"I have completed my ten tasks," said Heracles to King Eurystheus when he returned to Tiryns.

"You did not kill the Hydra alone," replied Eurystheus. "And the king paid you for cleaning the stables, which means you did the task for him. You have two more challenges. Fetch me Hera's golden apples."

Hera's golden apples grew on magic trees, hidden in a secret garden tended by nymphs. These were the children of a titan called Atlas.

Atlas lived on top of a mountain, holding the sky on his shoulders. He never moved, for fear the sky would slip off his back and crush the Earth.

"What brings you here, stranger?" he asked Heracles when the hero approached.

"I thought you might like company," said Heracles.

"It is indeed lonely here," replied Atlas.

"I am seeking Hera's golden apples," said Heracles. "Why don't you visit your children and bring me the fruit? I'll hold the sky up while you're gone."

The two changed places and Atlas set off.

"I want to see the world," he said to Heracles when he returned. "You can hold up the sky from now on."

"Wait," said Heracles. "I need to put on my cloak if I'm going to be here forever. Take the sky a moment."

Atlas took the sky again. Heracles laughed.

"Good-bye!" he said, snatching the basket of apples and walking away.

Cerberus, the Hound of Hell

"Your last task," said Eurystheus to Heracles, "is to bring me Cerberus, the three-headed dog that guards the entrance to the underworld!"

Heracles knew that Cerberus was the fiercest monster of all. How could he possibly capture him?

"Take a collar made of adamantine," suggested an old friend. "Fit it around his neck and you'll tame him."

Heracles found the entrance to the underworld. The three-headed dog spotted him and, opening all three mouths, unleashed a torrent of fire.

Heracles was wearing the magic lion skin so the flames did him no harm. This took Cerberus by surprise, giving Heracles time to leap onto his back. He snapped the collar around the monster's middle neck and the spell took hold. Cerberus fell asleep.

He did not even stir as Heracles dragged him by the tail all the way to Eurystheus's palace.

"You have killed the monster," said Eurystheus.

"He is only sleeping," said Heracles.

"Take him back to the underworld," cried the king. "You have completed your tasks, Heracles. You can go!"

On Mount Olympus, Zeus turned to Hera. "Do you agree now that Heracles is a brave hero?"

"Brave? Well, I suppose he has survived all of the challenges," admitted Hera.

Zeus smiled. "Heracles shall go down in history as the greatest hero of all time!"